DEAD ON TOAST

"I'd never seen a dead body before. Now I'm used to it.

You may not believe what I'm about to tell you. But the world will soon know the lot.

My blog will see to that."

DEATH

ON TOAST

Fifteen great
SHARP SHADES 2.0 *reads:*

DEATH
ON TOAST

John Townsend

Rans☺m

SHARP SHADES 2.0
Death on Toast
by John Townsend

Published by Ransom Publishing Ltd.
Unit 7, Brocklands Farm, West Meon, Hampshire GU32 1JN, UK
www.ransom.co.uk

ISBN   978 178127 991 5
First published in 2016

CONTENTS

Freddy's Blog
Saturday, 11.30

I'd never seen a dead body before.
Now I'm used to it.

You may not believe what I'm about
to tell you. But the world will soon
know the lot. My blog will see to that.

First of all, 3 *fast facts* about me:
1. I'm 14, but I'm not telling you my birthday. Just in case.
2. I'm Freddy and I live in the UK. No clues where. Just in case.
3. I've just seen a dead body. Human. Not in a movie. It's real and still warm. But I'm not telling you who. Not yet. Just in case.

Some of my blog might shock you. I'm going to put in secrets. I've got to tell it as it is. I just hope no one at school reads it. That would let the cat out of the bag.

Talking of cats, my Mum once

said I was like a tomcat. It wasn't from the smell in my room. It's because I keep myself to myself. I've always been a loner and that's just fine.

In fact, Mum said they should have a cat-flap fitted for me (a Freddy-flap). Then I could come and go as I like. In the end, they gave me a door key. I've had it since I was nine.

For five years I've been letting myself in and out when I want. That's because they're never here. I spend a lot of time alone. That suits me just fine. I'm not a weird teenage freak. Not really. It's just that I've always been a bit different.

We've never been a normal family. Three words sum up my parents: posh, busy and out. They're never here!

How cool is that? I can do just what I like. That's most kids' dream. Think what you'd do if you could always do what you liked.

I bet you'd like that, wouldn't you?

The only thing is, I now think it's not such a big deal after all. To be honest, it's all gone a bit pear-shaped.

I'm about to tell you just how bad the shape of a pear can get …

Sunday, 14.58

I didn't sleep last night. I watched
scary movies all night in my room.
I ate a tub of ice cream with toffee
chunks for breakfast. I'm still in bed
– with my phone. There's something

I've got to tell you. I can't keep it to myself any longer.

Until now I've always kept my secret in the family. Not that we're close … all wrapped up in our own worlds. Mum and Dad have never been as wrapped-up as they are right now.

I once told Mum I often felt lonely. She just kept putting on her lip-gloss.

'Don't be silly, Freddy. We live in a lovely country area and we've got a posh house. Dad is very rich and you've got all you want.'

For Christmas I gave them the

DVD of *Home Alone*. They didn't
see the joke.

'We have to work long hours to
give you all the things you like. You
cost us a fortune in food.'

That's a laugh. Food like Cuppa-
soup, Pot Noodles or tins of beans.
The freezer is full of dull ready-meals.

I don't know when we last had a
proper meal at the table. Not even
at Christmas. They went out, so I
ended up having a Cuppa-soup with
the dog.

I hate Sundays. I feel so yuk. It's
windy and raining. From here I can

see right down the garden. It's gross out there. Grey and cold. Just one bent flower by the compost heap. All alone. I know how it feels.

I've got a Maths test tomorrow. Yet another one. I don't care as I'm not going to school for a bit. I'll stay at home with my DVDs. I want to watch *Killer Kids from Kindergarten*.

Then I'll go online and order lots more horror movies and computer games. Cool.

They're all '18' but who's to know? Only you. You're not going to tell anyone, are you? You won't breathe a word.

I want you to promise.
Then I'll tell you my secret.

Tuesday, 00.14

I can't get to sleep. I keep hearing noises, but I know no one's here.

I should be used to being here alone all night. It's so creepy. I wish I hadn't watched *Zombie Flesh Eaters* before bed.

I spent hours online, too. I can
share my feelings and they stay
secret. No one knows who I am. I'm
just known as *fredblog*. It's always
been my username, but it means so
much more now. My little joke.

I get a bit upset at how things have
gone. I get upset about my spotty face,
too. I blame Mum. Her skin looks as
lumpy as bubble-wrap. I blame her for
passing on the spots gene.

I once said, 'It's good to keep
things in the family, eh, Mum?'

She was well upset and phoned
Kalvin.

He's her 'stress nurse'. He comes

in a rusty old van to give her a leg wax. Only when Dad's away. But I can't say any more.

Dad and I do most of the cleaning. Mum says she has to keep her hands smooth for her image.

She once sprayed bleach in the washing machine and said, 'Your dirty pants have been in there, Freddy.'

I tried to tell her my boxer shorts aren't atomic waste.

I said, 'Mum, you're the only woman I know who needs the sat-nav to find the tumble dryer. And to find a tad of time for your only son.'

She didn't smile.

Dad told me, 'You'll understand one day, Freddy. Your mother has a stressful job. She and I have to look tip-top and be seen in all the right places. That's why I go away a lot. Our faces have to be out there.'

I didn't say anything. I just squeezed one of my spots and dabbed on the zit gel.

Mum works in underwear. I don't mean that's all she wears. That would be gross. She has to go around buying knickers for M&S. I've often wished I could take her back and get a better fit – with a bit more time.

Dad's got a top job at Esso. Or so he says. At a big dinner party here he went on and on about how great he is in oil. So I said, 'So are sardines, but they don't brag about it.'

I was sent to my room.

Dad is such a know-all. He has to be right all the time. And he can never see the funny side. Like that time when I was ten and he took me to one side.

'Your mother says I need to talk to you, Freddy. About sex.'

'That's OK, Dad. What do you need to know?'

He went mad. I was grounded for

making fun of him. Worth it, though!

Dad has always told me off for silly stuff.

'Don't bite your nails!'

He does that all the time when he's driving the Jag. And if I ask why I have to do as I'm told, it's always those four words every adult says ...

'Because I say so.'

'Mum, why can't I stay the night at Robert's?'

'Because I said so.'

The real reason is, 'Because we'll have to have him back here and he's not posh enough.'

Friends are banned. They might leave a spec of dust on the carpet. I'm never allowed in the front room unless I take my shoes and socks off.

When she's not at work, Mum goes away on 'Spa Nights'. I asked her if they were to get rid of her double chin. She was well-mad and stormed out the house. Off to see Kalvin.

She gets all sulky each time she goes up a size. That's often.

Chips are banned here.

'Chips will give you more spots, Freddy.'

I tried to explain that I eat them,

not rub them in my face.

After she stepped off the scales with a scream, Mum snapped, 'Freddy, why is it you eat so much and stay so skinny? I hate you. I really hate you!'

I think she was only joking, but I gave her one of my scary stares with a twisted grin.

Just like the serial killer in *High School Bloodbath*.

Then I croaked in my best psycho voice, 'Not as much as I hate you, my dear ... '

You should have seen her face.

Thursday, 14.34

I've taken the day off again. I hate
school. I can't face it right now.

I blame Mum and Dad. They've
been getting to me lately.

I try to talk as if they're still here.

It seems best. But they won't come back now. They've gone for good.

It's been a month now. A whole month of living on my own – all by myself. Chips in bed. Sweets when I like. Shoes in the front room. Feet on the sofa. Pants left where I like. More money than I want. Any adult DVD I want to watch, when I like.

Life's a dream. Not a Cuppa-soup in sight.

It happened so quickly. I made up my mind when I came in the door and found yet another note telling me to open a tin of beans and be in bed by ten.

'We're away till Sunday. Make sure you wipe the sink after doing your spots – and leave the toilet seat DOWN.

'Keep the kitchen tidy and soak your pants in bleach. Don't forget to walk the dog, dig the garden and cut the lawn. Stay out of the front room.'

Something snapped inside me. A voice in my head said, 'Why do you put up with all this? Get rid of them, my dear … '

And when a voice says that, you just have to listen.

I'd always fancied running my own affairs. Now I can take charge of my own life. In fact, I can run this place better than them.

If only Miss Finch knew it was her who gave me the idea. Her Biology lessons are usually grim, but my eyes lit up when she held up a poster of the Death Cap Fungus. I just couldn't help thinking of Mum – and her weakness for garlic mushrooms.

That weekend I searched the woods at the end of the lane. There were masses of them. Their deadly heads poked above the fallen leaves. The page in my book said: '*Deadly toxic. Warning – looks like the edible mushroom.*'

So I fried some in butter and garlic. Dead tasty, without tasting deadly!

I mixed in something else from our garden. I'd better not say what, just in case a nutter reads this and tries it out. After all, there are some crazy kids about.

So, the mix went over a pizza – a topping to die for. Just the job.

I didn't think it would really work. Not so fast, anyway. What upset me most was Mum giving some to the dog. In minutes Sadie was flat out in the laundry room.

Dad was on his laptop and Mum

was eating a low-fat trifle. They didn't even notice the dog.

I was being given my orders: 'Freddy, we've stocked the freezer with low-fat ready-meals. We're both away for a few days. There are plenty of Cuppa-soups in the cupboard. Don't forget the rules. I've put a post-it note on your door to tell you what you can and can't do. What's that noise? I hope Sadie isn't being sick on the rug. Hurry up and eat your pizza and take your elbows off the t ... '

And that was it. She slumped with a gurgle. Face down in the trifle.

Dad went five minutes later. Out like a light – trying to phone the doctor.

It was such a struggle moving the bodies. They were heavy as lead. I waited till it was dark, of course. I got really muddy, but it didn't take long to get rid of them. Mum and Dad should be pleased. After all, they did tell me to dig the garden.

They'll never be found. Nor the dog. All wrapped in the duvet and under the compost heap. Quite deep, too. That was Miss Finch's idea. Her lesson on worms and maggots was her best yet.

I took the next day off school. After all, it's not every day you become an orphan. Besides, I had *The Demon Within* to watch. That's such a scary DVD.

No one suspects a thing. Everyone is used to me saying, 'Sorry, Dad's away at the moment,' or, 'Mum's on a training course,' or 'at the Health Club.'

I just deal with his emails. Online banking is a doddle. It's easy to pay bills that way. I transfer cash into my account if I need a few quid. After all, nobody knows you're a kid online.

I reply to texts and emails on Mum's phone and everyone thinks they're from her. I sent a text to Kalvin to let him know he was no longer needed. There were some odd replies to that one.

It was a pain when Mum's work kept emailing and phoning. I had to tell them she was leaving to care for a sick uncle in New Zealand. That shut them up. So it's all been a doddle so far.

Maybe I should have waited till Parents' Evening was over. It was easy forging the note to say they were ill, but Miss Finch asked questions.

Still, it's no big deal. Not all parents attend anyway. It wouldn't surprise me if half my class has done the same as me. It must be quite common.

I might go to school tomorrow. I'll see. I don't want them getting awkward and asking too many questions.

Mind you, I'd rather stay at home on my own. I love to watch gross DVDs on the wide-screen with the sound turned up full blast. Then the screams echo all round the house.

Call me sad, but it beats school.

I've got to log off now. I need to answer the phone. It's been ringing all day. Time for some more little white lies …

Wednesday, 22.48

Mum's work won't leave me alone. They don't like the *Uncle in New Zealand* story. Her boss says he smells a rat. He says he's going to call round. I haven't slept since.

Miss Finch upset me, too. She said she wanted a 'quiet word' after the lesson. She came straight out with it. Why didn't I have any friends? She said I was a loner and seemed a bit odd.

I just smiled – a sort of twisted grin. Then I gave a wink. That seemed to make her back off.

When I got home from school I checked Mum's emails. I think my plan worked. I'd sent her boss a message telling him what she thought of him. As an added extra, I said she was running away with

her secret lover at Head Office.
There haven't been any texts since,
so I reckon I'm safe.

I hope so.

Then came the bombshell. Just
when I thought I was off the hook,
who should appear on the doorstep?
Miss Finch!

I tried to keep calm and act
normal. I was churning inside, but
I didn't let it show. I had to hide the
beer I was drinking.

She looked at me oddly and said it
was time for a home visit from my
caring form teacher. She asked all

kinds of questions. Had I done my
Biology homework on fungi and
rotters? I told her she had no need to
worry as I'd done my own research
in the garden.

I took her into the front room.
I didn't care about her shoes, even
though they were muddy. She left a
mark on the carpet, but I said it
didn't matter.

'We're very relaxed in this house,'
I said. 'Mum and Dad have never
been so relaxed. Let me show you
round. I can tell you'd like a peep.'

She said. 'I had no idea you lived
out here in the wilds.'

'Yes,' I smiled. 'A classy area. Not even any neighbours for a lad to annoy.'

It felt weird showing my teacher round the crime scene. But it was kind of thrilling, too. I can't explain it – but I got a real buzz.

'What a posh kitchen,' she said. 'I'd die to have a kitchen like this.'

'Really?' I said. 'How interesting.'

Then she came out with it. What I'd been dreading all along. Could she speak to Mum or Dad?

'Things are very busy right now,' I lied. 'Mum's away. She's in Dublin.'

Miss Finch gave me a look, then went on and on. *I could talk to her at any time. Was I in trouble? Was I upset?*

'After all,' she said, with an odd stare, 'I know there's something wrong. I looked in the garage on my way in. Both your parents' cars are in there, aren't they?'

I told her we're a three-car family. Dad was out in the BMW.

That shut her up. But not for long. That's when she came out with her trump card.

'I popped into your Mum's work after school.'

'Really?' I said. 'Would you like a cup of tea while you wait?'

'They told me she'd left. All a bit strange. Something about New Zealand. Something about a man at Head Office.'

That's when I found my drama lessons came in handy. I put on a bit of an act and had a little cry. Just for effect. Nothing much. Just to put her at her ease.

I wiped my nose on the dishcloth and said, 'Mum and Dad have got such a lot on top of them at the moment. I'd like to tell you more, but I'd prefer to keep it in the family.'

'You can trust me, you know.'

'What if someone at school asks you why you came here?'

She looked quite hurt. 'No one knows I'm here. I came because I care, not because anyone sent me. I haven't even told my partner where I am.'

I smiled. 'I'd feel better if you joined me for a meal. I could talk to you better then.'

She gave me another look. 'If that would help. Can I do anything?'

'No, it's almost ready. I've just got to heat the soup and that's it.'

'It smells great. What sort of soup?'

'My favourite,' I said, chopping the mushrooms. 'Cream of mushroom.'

'I love mushrooms,' she said. 'Especially wild ones like those.'

'That's good,' I said. 'I'll give you some more on toast. Dead tasty. With garlic and something special from the garden.'

'That would be lovely,' she smiled.

While they sizzled in the pan, she looked out of the kitchen window. Down towards the compost heap.

'What a super garden. It must be rich soil.'

'Yes. A lot of body in it. Lots of

worms. I've done a bit of digging since your lesson on maggots. That compost heap is full of them now.'

She soon finished her soup – while I ate a ham roll. I told her what I'd done. Everything.

She didn't seem to hear what I was saying. She ate her mushrooms on toast in a daze, then gave an ugly stare.

'I hate these mushrooms,' she grunted.

I gave my evil laugh. The one from *Psycho Chainsaw*.

I croaked, 'Not as much as I hate you, my dear … '

She didn't seem to see the funny side.

I'd never heard a teacher groan like that before. It wasn't nice, I can tell you. She was still gurgling as she went in the wheelie-bin. By the time I'd pushed her down the garden, there wasn't a sound to be heard.

Apart from the first thud of the spade …

Friday, 04.37

I've been ill. Really bad. It's not from what I've eaten. That's because I haven't eaten a thing. Not since the ham roll when Miss Finch called.

I haven't slept much, either.

I dread this time of night. I feel sick in my bones.

I had a bit of a panic after I buried Miss Finch. Her car was the problem. I had to act fast to get rid of it. Well, I couldn't leave it down the track, could I? A red soft-top VW is a bit of a give-away. Especially with Year 9 Biology books on the back seat.

It was after midnight when I sat in the car. I turned the key and the car came to life. A gentle purr drifted through the mist. I let off the handbrake and pressed down the clutch. Then I crunched into first gear.

The car shot forward and jolted along the track. I tried to work the clutch and change gear. It wasn't the best of rides. I didn't turn on the lights – just in case. The moon let me see where I was going. It wasn't far.

I skidded up the track through the trees. Then I turned off in a clearing and slid over the mud. Up to the top of the old quarry. It was very spooky there. So I flicked on the headlights. Mist swirled in the beam.

My heart was beating like a drum. I pressed a button and the roof slid back with a whisper. I stared up at the stars. Moonlight spilled across the Biology books on the back seat. I pulled on the handbrake and switched off the engine. As I got out of the car you could hear a pin drop.

I stepped forward very slowly – towards the edge. My toes jutted over the cliff-top. I peered down to the deep, shimmering lake … silver beneath the moon. I took a deep breath, got back in the car and let off the handbrake. I flicked off the lights, ran to the back bumper and pushed.

Slowly the car moved forward, till the front tyres rolled over the edge.

I fell in the mud as the car glided out into space. It seemed to give a sigh as it hung in mid air, before dropping. I gasped as shrill music filled the night. It drifted up from the dark shape falling towards the lake.

Miss Finch's phone! I should have switched it off. I should have checked.

I swore … just as the night filled with a roar. The car plunged below the silver spray.

The echo died, the water swirled and the lake closed over. It was soon as smooth as glass once more … shivering beneath the moon.

I turned, gave a sigh and walked back down the track. I felt very calm again. Relief, like the mist, swirled around me. Only the moon knew my secret now.

Or so I thought.

Monday, 02.51

I slept for two days and nights.
I think. I've lost all track of time.
  I blame Mum's sleeping pills. They
knocked me out. Till the scream
woke me. It was my own scream.

Then I heard voices. Mum's and Dad's. They seemed to be calling from the compost heap.

I keep seeing Miss Finch slumped in the laundry room. I hear groaning coming from the wheelie-bin. I feel Sadie lick my hand whenever I shut my eyes. I know it's all in my mind, but it's really weird.

To be honest, I'm scared. I'm too scared to watch DVDs any more.

I've got a box set of *Psychic Devil* to see, but I just can't face it. I feel like there's a DVD always running in my head. But I can't turn it off.

I bet I won't sleep tonight. It will

take me ages to check my blog. The secret I've just written is about to go live. I can't wait to see if anyone posts a comment. I need someone to tell me I'll be OK.

I don't regret what I've done. Not really. Apart from the voices in my head. I keep shaking, too. It's always there in my sleep – the smell of garlic mushrooms. I wake feeling sick. I can't wash away that smell.

My nightmares are always the same. I'm driving a red car as it falls through the night with a phone ringing in the mist … as a hand

grabs me. Then I hear the whisper.

Someone out there knows the truth. A voice on the phone whispers my name. It says the police can trace a phone exactly. They know where the car is. They're watching me.

That's why I wake screaming. That's what makes me sick. That's why I'm scared. I can't keep my secret to myself any more. It's killing me.

That's why I've done the blog. I had to. You see, you're helping me.

I need to tell someone – to get it off my mind.

I'm not stupid. I've changed all the names in this blog. I'm not really called Freddy. Even Sadie isn't her real name. I'm not totally mad.

No one will ever know who I am. All you know is my username – *fredblog*. You've no idea where I live.

After all, we're always warned never to give away who we really are – so I'm not going to. The police won't know who *fredblog* is. The *blog.com* is my joke. Dot Com is a code. DOT stands for Death On Toast. COM is Cream Of Mushroom. Funny, eh?

If you read this blog, I wonder if you think I did the right thing. I'm not that bad really – am I?

At first I wasn't going to send this at all. I'll delete it from my phone so there'll be no trace. No one can prove I wrote it if I bury my phone.

The worst has just happened. It's the moment I've been dreading – my worst fear. It's way past midnight. I'm still in the house alone. I'm sitting here shivering. I've been on my Xbox for hours … but now there's hammering on the front

door. Drumming through my head.
Thumping like my heart. Pounding
through my body …

I'm not going to answer. Never.
They'll have to come and get me.
Their blue light is flashing through
my curtains. It's sweeping around
the room. It's swirling across the
screen. My eyes can't focus. I can
hear them calling my name.

It's all over. At last. I'll send this
and wait. I'm about to click on
'post'. Then at least someone will
know the truth … YOU.

PS Please keep this to yourself.
Don't tell a soul. It's our secret.

Feel free to post a comment. And just let me know if you want any scary DVDs.

All harmless fun.
Up to a point.